Happy 5th Birthday,
Sophia!

We love you!

Love
Auntie Kim, Uncle Frank
Anthony, Nicholas, Courtney & Danielle

♡

The Train to Maine

Down East Books

Text copyright © 2008 by Jamie Spencer
Illustrations copyright © 2008 by Rebecca Harrison Reed

Printed in Johor, Malaysia, June 2014

ISBN: 978-0-89272-767-4

Down East Books
www.nbnbooks.com
Distributed by
National Book Network
800-462-6420

Library of Congress Cataloging-in-Publication Data: Spencer, Jamie.
  The train to Maine / story by Jamie Spencer ; illustrations by Rebecca Reed.
when one arrives "down east."
    p. cm.
  Summary: In rhyming text, describes the sights along the train ride from Boston to Maine, as well as the fun things to be done
                                                                                    itle.

  ISBN 978-0-89272-767-4 (trade hardcover : alk. paper)
  [1. Stories in rhyme. 2. Railroad trains--Fiction. 3. Massachusetts--Fiction. 4. Maine--Fiction.] I. Reed, Rebecca, ill. II. T
  PZ8.3.S7493Tr 2008
  [E]--dc22
                                    2007039498

For T., who wanted to know where the train went.
—J.S.

For Justin, Ed, Pat, and Emily.
—R.H.R.

Every day at quarter past noon
the tracks start to hum with a traveling tune.
With a whir and a whoosh and a clickety-clack,
the train to Maine roars down the track.

Over the trestle, high in the sky,
its sleek silver cars go streaking on by.
It doesn't stop, doesn't even slow down.
The train to Maine just rushes through town.

O' the train to Maine is Portland bound.

From Boston that's up, but to Maine we go down.

We'll wade in the waves, have a lobster feast,

riding north out of Boston, heading Down East.

Down at the station, we find the track.

We head down the platform, our bags all packed.

The conductor greets us, gives his hat a tip,

punching our tickets with a brisk snip-snip.

We leave North Station at 12 o'clock,
chugging slowly at first, then the cars start to rock.
Past honking drivers and jammed traffic lanes,
leaving Boston in the dust, on our way to Maine.

On the train to Maine, we're Portland bound.
From Boston it's up, but to Maine we go down.
We'll catch a sea breeze to beat the heat,
riding north out of Boston, heading Down East.

We race along, engine starting to purr
as southbound freight cars go by in a blur.
We roar past a playground, a station, a square,
over a trestle, high in the air.

The train whistle blows as a crossing nears,
warning cars and trucks to settle their gears.
Drivers line up at the flashing sign
as the train to Maine speeds down the line.

On the train to Maine, we're vacation bound.
From Boston it's up, but to Maine we go down.
We'll laze on a lake, gobble blueberry treats,
riding north out of Boston, heading Down East.

Rails hug the curves of a riverside
through criss-cross girders of a bridge so wide.
High above water, the wheels whoosh along,
slick tracks singing a traveling song.

Birch trees shimmer 'gainst a clear blue sky
as white-spired steeples go flickering by.
Leaving mill towns and smokestacks far behind,
we're headed north with Maine on our minds.

On the train to Maine, we're adventure bound.
From Boston it's up, but to Maine we go down.
We'll fish from a skiff, catch a deep sea beast,
riding north out of Boston, heading Down East.

EXETER

Exeter, Durham, and Dover, too—
the conductor calls out stations, clear and true.
All down the train, we hear him shout,
calling "Dover, Dover, this way out!"

DOVER

NEW HAMPSHIRE

N H

DURHAM

Passengers hurry to climb inside,
eager to join us on our Maine-bound ride.
With a wave, the conductor gives the OK,
and the train to Maine rolls on its way.

On the train to Maine, we're Portland bound.

From Boston it's up, but to Maine we go down.

We'll sail on a ship, skim the sunlit seas,

riding north out of Boston, heading Down East.

Next stop, Wells, Saco, Old Orchard Beach.
The end of the line is nearly in reach.
Then a glimpse of the sea down a narrow lane,
"Hooray, hooray! At last we're in Maine!"

Ocean waves beckon, smell the sea air,

'Cross a long, low bridge and we'll soon be there.

Portland comes into view on a high hilltop,

as the train to Maine sloooows to a stop.

On the train from Maine, we're homeward bound.
Our time is up, we're winding down.
We'll watch out the windows, maybe catch some Zs,
riding south of Portland and dreaming Down East.

The Meaning of "Down East"

Although the State of Maine lies north of Massachusetts, parts of the Maine coast stretch out to the east past Boston. Long ago, when ships plied the coastal waters off New England, sailors traveling from Boston to Maine used to say they were heading "Down East," because they had to sail down wind (with the wind at their backs) to get there. Returning to Boston required sailing into the wind, or upwind, so sailors spoke of going "up to Boston."

The "Downeaster" train is Amtrak's rail service between Boston, Massachusetts and Portland, Maine. The trip takes less than two-and-a-half hours, one way.